by Lea Taddonio illustrated by Mina Price
Head over Heels
First Date
Spellbound
An Imprint of Magic Wagon
abdopublishing.com

To PB &J, my favorite combo —LT

For Lindsay —MP

abdopublishing.com

Published by Magic Wagon, a division of ABDO, PO Box 398166,
Minneapolis, Minnesota 55439. Copyright © 2017 by Abdo
Consulting Group, Inc. International copyrights reserved in all
countries. No part of this book may be reproduced in any form
without written permission from the publisher. Spellbound™ is a
trademark and logo of Magic Wagon.

Printed in the United States of America, North Mankato, Minnesota.
102016
012017

**THIS BOOK CONTAINS
RECYCLED MATERIALS**

Written by Lea Taddonio
Illustrated by Mina Price
Edited by Heidi M.D. Elston
Art Directed by Candice Keimig
Series lettering and graphics from iStockphoto

Publisher's Cataloging-in-Publication Data

Names: Taddonio, Lea, author. | Price, Mina, illustrator.
Title: First date / by Lea Taddonio ; illustrated by Mina Price.
Description: Minneapolis, MN : Magic Wagon, 2017. | Series: Head over heels ; Book 2
Summary: Lola Jones is going on her first date with C.J Kline, the star point guard of the
   Washington Warcats basketball team. But can they keep their plans secret from Lola's
   big brother and C.J's best friend?
Identifiers: LCCN 2016947639 | ISBN 978162402193 (lib. bdg.) | ISBN 9781624022531
   (ebook) | ISBN 9781624022838 (Read-to-me ebook)
Subjects: LCSH: High school students--Juvenile fiction. | Best friends--Juvenile fiction. |
   Interpersonal relationships--Juvenile fiction. | Human behavior--Juvenile fiction.
Classification: DDC [Fic]--dc23
LC record available at http://lccn.loc.gov/2016947639

Table
of
Contents

Out of This World

Before school
I go to my locker.
There is a note taped
to the door that
says "*Lola.*"
I don't know the
handwriting.

"Morning!" My
best friend Kizzie
walks up and points.
"Who's **THAT** from?"

4

6

"No clue."

I open it up. Inside the envelope are three heart-shaped pictures cut from a magazine. One is a picture of a **starry sky**. Another is a picture of a **bowling ball**. The last is a picture of *ice cream*.

There is also a note. A shiver goes through my body.

Dear Lola,

Will you go out with me? If the answer is yes, then choose our first date:

1. We visit the planetarium (because you are out of this world)

2. We go bowling (because you knock me down)

3. We get ice cream (because you are so sweet)

Text me your answer at (555) 423 - 1980.

Love,
C.J

"Girl, what does it say?" Kizzie jumps up and down. "Tell me! Tell me!"

I open my mouth, but no words come out. Is this a dream? But when I blink again, I'm still standing in the school hallway.

Kizzie rips the note from my hands and SCREAMS. "I don't know if I can say yes," I whisper.

"SORRY." She puts her hand to her ear. "Did I hear you right?"

"My brother warned me never to look at one of his basketball teammates. C.J is his *BEST FRIEND*."

"What Joseph doesn't know won't **hurt** him." Kizzie says. "What matters is if you want that **date**."

I know the answer. **"YES."**

Worst Date Ever

I choose the planetarium. I didn't know what it was and had to look up the word on my phone. It's like a **MOVIE THEATER**, except you learn about the stars and other objects in the night sky.

It sounded *cool*. Plus, sitting in the dark sounds easier than talking.

C.J meets me at the train station on Friday night. We have to go all the way **DOWNTOWN**. He looks *so* good. Instead of his usual jersey and sweat pants, he wears a nice shirt and dark jeans. I don't know why, but **seeing** him in dressier clothes makes me even more *nervous*.

He sits across from me
on the **TRAIN**. "How was
DRUM LINE practice?"

"Okay," I say. Our high school marching band is one of the **BEST** in the state. Our new routine is **HARD**, and all I do is practice. But I don't tell him that. I don't say *anything* else.

"*Cool*," he says at last.

We look out the window. The neighborhood **CHANGES**. The buildings get **BIGGER**. More people get on wearing business clothes.

We aren't talking. He isn't having fun. *Oh no!* This is the worst date **EVER**.

It's Just Me

"This is our stop." C.J stands up. I'm **surprised** he still wants to go through with this. I'm being so *shy* that it would make sense if he wanted to call off the date.

When we get outside, he *touches* my arm. "Hey, can I be **STRAIGHT** with you?"

24

My mouth goes **dry**.

"Yeah. Sure."

"It's just me, Lola." He **smiles**. "The same guy that hangs out at your house **EVERY** weekend."

"I know." I can't stop **looking** at his smile.

"All I'm saying is that you seem **nervous**."

I **SHRUG**.

He *KICKS* at the sidewalk.
"It's cool. I'm ᴨᴇʀᴠᴏᴜꜱ too."
I *jerk*. "You? Why?"

He rubs his hair. "It's not every day I hang out with the **prettiest** girl from Washington High."

Before I can think, he takes my hand. His skin is **WARM**. "I've been working up the **COURAGE** to ask you out since school started. You aren't the only one who gets *shy*."

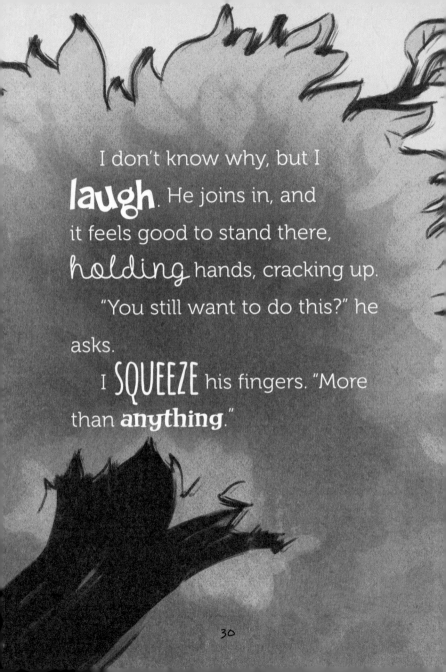

I don't know why, but I **laugh**. He joins in, and it feels good to stand there, *holding* hands, cracking up.

"You still want to do this?" he asks.

I **SQUEEZE** his fingers. "More than **anything**."

Walking on Air

It turns out that C.J.'s cousin Marcus is a SCIENCE teacher at the planetarium. He gets us the best seats. The room is DARK. The chairs tip back, and the ceiling CURVES.

"I've *never* been here," C.J says.

"Why not?" I ask.

"Guess I wanted to take someone *special*," he says in a **low** voice.

Before I do anything but turn **bright** red, the lights go out. A MILLION stars appear on the ceiling. C.J's knee is right *next to* mine.

Marcus tells different **stories** people have made up about the stars. It's hard to pay **ATTENTION**.

C.J leans *close*. His breath makes my ear warm. "Are you having a nice time?"

"The **BEST**," I whisper back.

He brushes a hair off my cheek. "The stars are *beautiful*, but it's better watching *you*."

If I felt any happier, I'd EXPLODE.

After the show ends, we walk to the lakeshore and watch the **sunset**. He buys us hot dogs in the **PARK**. The train ride home isn't *quiet*. This time we can't stop **talking**.

It turns out we both like **ACTION** movies and *jazz*. Our favorite food is **MACARONI AND CHEESE**. We both are at practice all the time.

He says he likes watching me **play** drums at halftime. I tell him I always **CHEER** loudest for him at the games.

When we walk back into our **NEIGHBORHOOD**, it's like I'm not on the sidewalk. I'm walking on **AIR**.

"I had a *nice* time," I say when we reach my street.

He **frowns**. "You aren't going to let me walk you home?"

"I don't want **DRAMA** with my brother. You know how he is." Joseph is my **BIG** brother, but *sometimes* he acts like my dad.

"Lola." C.J is *quiet* for a second. "I **like** being with you. And I think you **like** being with me."

I study my **shoes**. "I do."

"Then we have to tell Joseph about us. I want more *dates* with you, but he is my friend. I don't like going **BEHIND HIS BACK**."

"I will," I promise. "Soon."

He nods. "All right. I'll see you at the **GAME** tomorrow night."

As I walk home, I *smile* thinking about my **happy** memories from tonight. Will my big brother ever be cool with me *dating* his ***BEST FRIEND***?